MAYBE TOMORROW?

BY **CHARLOTTE AGELL**

ILLUSTRATED BY **ANA RAMÍREZ GONZÁLEZ**

SCHOLASTIC PRESS · NEW YORK

ELBA had a big block.
She'd been dragging it
around for a long time.

It made her walk slowly.
It made her think darkly.
It was heavy.

NORRIS danced everywhere he went, even uphill.

One day, Elba was sitting on her block
in the park, like she usually did.

Along came Norris in a cloud of butterflies.
At first Elba couldn't see him in all that shininess.

"Hello, I'm Norris," he said.
"Do you want to go on a picnic?"
"I'm Elba," said Elba. "I do not go on picnics."
"Well, what do you want to do?" asked Norris.
"Sit here with my block."

"But you're already doing that."
"I know."
"Is it fun?"
"Not really. No."

"What's IN it?" Norris wanted to know.
"In it?" said Elba. "What do you mean?"
"Well, it's a BOX, isn't it?
Something must be inside it."

"It's not a box, it's a BLOCK," said Elba.
"Are you sure?" asked Norris.
"Yes," said Elba, prodding it with her umbrella.
She always carried one, in case it rained.

Norris sat down next to Elba.
"I feel something in there," he said.
"What?" asked Elba, who didn't feel a thing.
"Something sad," said Norris.
"I think it wants to come out."
"How?" whispered Elba.

Norris and Elba sat there thinking.
The butterflies flitted this way and that.
"Maybe tomorrow," said Norris as the sun set.
"Maybe," said Elba.

The next day, it was raining.
The butterflies looked a little damp.

The weather didn't slow down Norris, though!
"You're making me dizzy," said Elba.
"It's time for tea," said Norris.

They had good, quiet tea with rain in it.

"Maybe tomorrow?" said Norris.
"Maybe," said Elba, "if tomorrow ever comes."

Tomorrow didn't come, but another today did.
"It's really time," said Norris, "because I want you
to come to the ocean with me."

"Okay, I'll just take my block," said Elba, surprising herself.
"But it's too heavy," she added. "Right?"
"My butterflies and I will help you," said Norris.

They did help.
It was a very, very long journey.
Elba and Norris talked and didn't talk.

"I miss Little Bird," said Elba
as they crested the last hill.
"She is gone."

"I miss her, too," said Norris.
Elba paused.
"But you didn't know her."
"No, but you are my friend,
so I can help you miss her."

By the time they got to the shore,
Norris knew many things about Little Bird.

"We watched the moon together," Elba said.
"She taught me to sing. We were hardly ever apart."

"She loved you so much," Norris said.

"Yes," said Elba as the waves crashed.

Some of the butterflies started to fly out toward the horizon.

"COME BACK!" shouted Elba.

"It's okay," said Norris. "Sometimes, we have to let things go."

They both sat down
to rest on Elba's block.
But there wasn't enough room!

"I think it's smaller," said Elba
in amazement. "And lighter."
"Definitely," agreed Norris.

Together they stood and faced the roaring sea.

"I'll always have this block, you know," said Elba.

"Yes, maybe you will," said Norris.

"But I will help you carry it sometimes."

The two friends stayed by the ocean
until the sun set and the view was calm.
Some of the butterflies came back.
Some flew off forever.

THANK YS

The next day was sunny.
"Do you want to go on a picnic?" Norris asked.
"YES," said Elba.

TO MY FAMILY,

NEAR AND FAR.

—CHARLOTTE

TO MY FRIENDS AND FAMILY. YOUR

LOVE AND KINDNESS ALWAYS HELP ME

FIND PEACE AND HEAL MY SOUL. —ANA

Text copyright © 2019 by Charlotte Agell • Illustrations copyright © 2019 by Ana Ramírez González • All rights reserved. Published by Scholastic Press, an imprint of Scholastic Inc., *Publishers since 1920*. SCHOLASTIC, SCHOLASTIC PRESS, and associated logos are trademarks and/or registered trademarks of Scholastic Inc. • The publisher does not have any control over and does not assume any responsibility for author or third-party websites or their content. • No part of this publication may be reproduced, stored in a retrieval system, or transmitted in any form or by any means, electronic, mechanical, photocopying, recording, or otherwise, without written permission of the publisher. For information regarding permission, write to Scholastic Inc., Attention: Permissions Department, 557 Broadway, New York, NY 10012. • This book is a work of fiction. Names, characters, places, and incidents are either the product of the author's imagination or are used fictitiously, and any resemblance to actual persons, living or dead, business establishments, events, or locales is entirely coincidental. • Library of Congress Cataloging-in-Publication Data available • ISBN 978-1-338-21488-8 • 10 9 8 7 6 5 4 3 2 1   19 20 21 22 23 • Printed in China 38 • First edition, April 2019 Ana Ramírez González's artwork was created with watercolors, charcoal, graphite, and a combination of traditional and digital brushes. • The text type was set in 16-pt. Adobe Garamond Pro Regular. • The display type was set in KG What The Teacher Wants. • The title type was hand-lettered by Ana Ramírez González. • The book was printed on 157 gsm Golden Sun Matte and bound at RR Donnelly Asia. • Production was overseen by Angie Chen. • Manufacturing was supervised by Shannon Rice. The book was art directed and designed by Marijka Kostiw and edited by Tracy Mack.